World of Reading

THIS IS BLACK WIDOW

Written by Clarissa Wong

Illustrated by Andrea Di Vito and Peter Pantazis

Based on the Marvel comic book series The Avengers

MARVEL

Los Angeles
New York

marvelkids.com

© 2015 MARVEL

Printed in the United States of America
First Edition, January 2015
1 3 5 7 9 10 8 6 4 2
G658-7729-4-14339
ISBN 978-1-4847-2517-7

SUSTAINABLE
FORESTRY
INITIATIVE

Certified Chain of Custody
Promoting Sustainable Forestry

www.sfiprogram.org ·
SFI-01415

The SFI label applies to the text stock

This is Natasha.

She is a secret agent.
She is also a spy.
She works for S.H.I.E.L.D.

She was an orphan.
She lived at the Red Room.

The Red Room was a secret camp.
It was an evil place.

The camp leaders trained
her to be a spy.
They taught her to steal.
She knew the Red Room was bad.

The Red Room was hurting people.
Natasha wanted to help people.
She wanted to fight for good.

She decided to join S.H.I.E.L.D. At first Nick Fury was unsure about her.

He knew she was good at spying.
Was she spying on him?
He wanted to make sure
she was telling the truth.

She helped the Avengers
stop the Red Room.
She led the Avengers
to the bad people.

Then Nick Fury could
trust Natasha.
He let her join S.H.I.E.L.D.
Her code name was Black Widow.

She wears black so no one notices her.
Black is also her favorite color.

Tony Stark gave her a weapon.
It is called the Widow's Bite.
It looks like bracelets.
But it is much more.

Watch out!
They shoot blasts.

Black Widow is quiet.
Black Widow is quick.

Black Widow is a good fighter.
She doesn't need Tony's help.
She can fight off aliens by herself!

She can flip in the air
and land on her feet.

She can kick high.

She can throw a good punch, too.
Look out!
She is prepared for anything.

She is good at hiding.

She can blend in with the crowd.

Can you find her?

She has red hair.

She is clever.
She can outsmart villains—no
matter how much bigger they are!

Just watch.
Black Widow kicks butt!

Black Widow can sneak into
any building.
She knows how to get in and out.
Nobody notices her.

She finds clues for S.H.I.E.L.D.
The clues help S.H.I.E.L.D. solve
many cases.

She helps the Avengers, too.
She is part of the team.

Natasha is good friends
with Hawkeye.
They are partners.
They work well together.

Black Widow is not always spying.
She practices ballet.
She is a graceful dancer.

Her ballet moves
help her in combat.
She can move with ease.

When she falls,
she picks herself up.

She never gives up.

She is the best at what she does.
She is Black Widow!